The Return of Light

A CHRISTMAS TALE

DIA CALHOUN

DRAWINGS BY LISA FALKENSTERN

MARSHALL CAVENDISH

Text copyright © 2007 by Dia Calhoun
Illustrations © 2007 by Marshall Cavendish

Marshall Cavendish Corporation
99 White Plains Road
Tarrytown, NY 10591
www.marshallcavendish.us/kids

Library of Congress Cataloging-in-Publication Data
Calhoun, Dia.
The Return of Light: a Christmas tale / by Dia Calhoun. — 1st ed.
p. cm.
Summary: When the Christmas Deer chooses Treewing, a five-year-old tree,
for the Christmas harvest, he is surprised since it is a year early, but is told
he has been picked for a special destiny.
ISBN 978-0-7614-5360-4
[1. Christmas—Fiction. 2. Christmas treesvFiction.] I. Title. II. Title:
Christmas tale.
PZ7.C12747Re 2007
[Fic]—dc22
2006100136

The text of this book is set in Mrs. Eaves.
Book design by Anahid Hamparian
Editor: Margery Cuyler

Printed in China
First edition
10 9 8 7 6 5 4 3 2 1

mc Marshall Cavendish

Acknowledgments

I would like to thank my agent, Steven Chudney; my editor, Margery Cuyler; and my colleagues Kathryn O. Galbraith, Lorie Ann Grover, Joan Holub, and Laura Kvasnosky for their help with this book. Special thanks to my husband, Shawn R. Zink

For James Ringlien and Jessie Ringlien,
two of my favorite jollies

Contents

One

THE PROMISE

WHEN BELLS JINGLED on the north side of Faith Mountain, the wind carried the sound over the ridge to Liefson's Christmas Tree Farm. There, beneath the fierce winter starlight, the trees lifted their branches.

"What's that?" cried Treewing. "Is it? . . . Could it be? . . ."

"Hush. Listen!" said Longbough.

The bells rang louder.

"The Christmas Deer is coming," the Eldest Trees whispered, both eager and afraid.

"Christmas is coming at last!" shouted Longbough. He swayed joyfully. He was an Elder, six years old—a year older than Treewing. On the far side of the farm, the seedling trees whimpered with fear and awe. They had never seen the Christmas Deer before.

"There he is!" cried Treewing.

With flying leaps, the Christmas Deer bounded over the ridge, spraying snow left and right. His antlers branched into twelve magnificent points. A star burned on the tip of each one. When the Christmas Deer stopped in front of the trees, the bells on his harness fell silent. His gray-muzzled head turned from side to side, and his hooves scraped the snow. He walked toward the first of the Eldest Trees.

Treewing's needles tingled.

The Christmas Deer stopped in front of Dewsylva, a six-year-old blue spruce.

"I promise," the Christmas Deer said to her, "that your life will bring The Return of Light to the humans." And he bowed his head and touched Dewsylva with his starry antlers. Light curled across her boughs. It whisked along each branch and twig and needle until she sparkled from trunk to tip. "Now you are a Christmas Tree," he added.

Then the Christmas Deer touched the next tree and the next—Longbough, Barkcone, Greenlyn, and Needleskip— changing all 199 of the Eldest into Christmas trees, promising that their lives would bring The Return of Light. Soon a glowing path of trees stretched across the hillside. It looked as though the Milky Way had come down to earth.

This was the fifth time Treewing had heard the bells and seen the Christmas Deer. Though Treewing was tall, he needed to grow one more year before the Christmas Deer turned him into a Christmas tree. He sighed. A year seemed a long time to wait.

After the Christmas Deer finished touching all the Eldest, he did something surprising. He walked back down Treewing's row. When he reached Treewing, the Christmas Deer stopped and turned his head. With eyes deep and brown and soft, he looked at Treewing. "My child," he said slowly, the words dancing on the frosty air. "You have a special destiny." The Christmas Deer bowed his head, touched Treewing with his starry antlers, and gave him the promise, turning him into a Christmas tree.

Treewing felt a thrill of joy and love as

light surged through him, swirling across his branches, along his trunk, and down to even the smallest of his roots. His sap sang and seemed to turn pure gold. Every inch of him felt more alive than ever before.

The Christmas Deer trotted down the row and leaped back up Faith Mountain. The stars on his antlers glimmered in and out of the towering firs on the ridge. His jingling bells grew fainter and fainter. Then he was gone, until next year, and the night was silent again.

Treewing stood in shock as the light faded from his branches. The Christmas Deer had touched him, given him the promise. Him. A five-year-old. Why? Such a thing had never happened before in all the long memory of the trees. The trees chattered, wondering what it meant.

"The Christmas Deer made a mistake by touching Treewing," said Barkcone, a six-year-old noble pine. "He's only five years old."

"Wolves and icicles!" exclaimed Longbough. "The Christmas Deer is all wise. All powerful. All seeing. He would never make a mistake."

"I have a special destiny," Treewing whispered. What did that mean? Surely something wonderful. He swelled with pride because the Christmas Deer had singled him out.

For the rest of the night, the Eldest Trees celebrated, singing songs that had been passed down for many generations. They sang of the children who would soon play around them. They sang of the silver and gold ornaments, the tinsel, garlands, and toys that would hang from their branches. They sang of the crystal stars that would crown their tips.

Last of all, the Eldest sang of ending the dark days of winter and bringing back the light of spring—The Return of Light. Longbough's voice boomed loudest of all. Tomorrow he and the other Eldest would leave for Christmas, for the beautiful world in the songs. Treewing longed to go with them, until he remembered that Mr. Liefson had to cut them down first.

Two

ONE SHORT

AT DAWN TREEWING woke to the sound of a giant truck rumbling up Faith Mountain. To the west, the sky burned purple as the sun rose above the ridge where the Christmas Deer had disappeared the night before.

One Short

"Bright morning, Treewing, my friend," Longbough said. "The snowbirds are searching for seeds on the bare ground beneath your trunk."

Treewing counted twelve birds. Birds always flocked around him—which was how he had come by his name. A nest leftover from last summer perched in his upper branches.

"I shall never see another sunrise on Faith Mountain," Longbough said sadly. "Nor shall I ever see you again, Treewing. Today is my Harvesting Day." A moment later, he shook his branches and was happy again. "Then I journey to Christmas!"

"Are you scared of the harvesting?" Treewing asked.

"No! Well, perhaps a little. A smidgen. A dab. But they say the Christmas Deer's touch keeps us from feeling the chain saws. And just think, Treewing, my dreams are finally coming true. I have been waiting for

Christmas a very long time. You are too young to understand."

The giant truck bellowed louder, rolling into sight, smoke puffing from its stack. Its four chained wheels clawed at the icy road. Even though Treewing knew it was not coming for him, he trembled so hard that snow fell from his branches.

The Liefsons started the chain saws and began harvesting the Eldest. While the high mechanical whine shrilled, the snowbirds flew up. They wheeled, then streaked like a black ribbon toward the ridge. Smoke clogged the air, and wood flesh spewed from the tree trunks. Longbough stood bravely, singing and laughing even as he fell. After all of the Eldest had been cut, the Liefsons bound their branches and loaded them into the mouth of the giant truck.

"Good-bye! Merry Christmas!" called Treewing and the other trees still left on the mountain.

One Short

The Eldest shouted back "Farewell!" as the Liefsons began to close the truck doors. Treewing stretched his roots into the soil just to feel how wonderful it was to be part of the earth.

A man clambered out of the giant truck and walked over to the Liefsons. Each time he swung his arms, the sleeves of his black jacket bunched up, showing wrists as thick as stumps.

"The deal was two hundred trees," he said. "You're one short."

"We lost some to lightning," Mrs. Liefson said, pulling down her baseball cap, "and some to the ice storm last week."

"Too bad." The man spat into the saw-dust-speckled snow. "But it's not my problem. The contract said two hundred. Now you get me one more, or I start unloading the ones I have."

The Liefsons looked at one another.

"All right." Mr. Liefson tapped his

upper lip. "You can have one of the five-year-olds. But it won't be worth as much as the others."

"That's the best we can do," added Mrs. Liefson.

"Then do it, and let me get back to my coffee." The man lumbered toward the giant truck.

Mr. Liefson picked up the chain saw and began walking down the rows, searching for a tall five-year-old tree.

"Oh!" exclaimed Leaflinda, a noble pine. "I wonder if he's going to choose Treewing."

"Yes, yes!" the other trees cried. "That must be why the Christmas Deer touched Treewing! It wasn't a mistake after all. It was so he could be cut down a year early."

Cut down! Treewing shivered. Could it be true? "You have a special destiny," the Christmas Deer had told him. But what was it?

Why should he be harvested a year early? Then Treewing's boughs lifted. He could journey to Christmas now! Today! He would not have to wait another long year. And yet, part of him knew that he was not ready, he was too young, he needed more time to grow. . . .

"This one," Mr. Liefson said, stopping beside him, raising the chain saw.

Although his branches trembled, Treewing stood tall and didn't flinch as the chain saw cut into his trunk. Treewing felt no pain. Golden dust from his body sprayed across the trampled snow. Then he was falling down, down, down, until—*smack*! He struck the ground. Mr. Liefson bound his branches and tossed him into the giant truck, which roared away from Faith Mountain.

Three

LOLLY'S CHRISTMAS TREE LOT

Treewing jolted awake as someone lifted him out of the giant truck and threw him onto the hard, black ground. He struggled against the ropes cutting into his boughs. His roots tingled, even though he knew they were far away on Faith Mountain.

A woman picked him up. A fuzzy pink beret squatted on her gray hair. A matching pink muffler dangled down her orange parka, and the fringe rippled against her violet jeans. She placed Treewing in one corner of a big square frame on the ground. The other three corners already held trees, each slightly tipped. There were so many frames, set in row after row, that the trees seemed to form a strange sort of forest. The woman snipped Treewing's ropes and spread out his branches. He started to stretch, but she turned him around and around until he grew dizzy.

"Alicia!" she called. A younger woman with spiky black hair popped her head between two trees in the next row.

"Yeah, Lolly?"

"I need some advice. Does this side look best?"

Alicia squinted at Treewing. "Turn it ninety degrees to the right. Yeah, there."

Lolly backed up, looking Treewing up and down. "A bit small, but it's got nice evenly spaced whorls. Still, we'll have to drop the price some."

"Hey," Alicia said. "Wait a minute. What's that up near the top of the tree? Stuffed back in the branches?"

"Where?" Lolly asked. "Oh, I see it." She reached into Treewing's branches and lifted out the bird's nest. "I'll throw it out."

"No!" cried Treewing. "Don't take that!"

"Give it to me," Alicia said. "It's exquisite."

Lolly put the nest in Alicia's hands, and Alicia carried it away.

Treewing's branches drooped.

Lolly sighed and pinched the bridge of her nose between her thumb and forefinger.

"I'm so tired," she whispered. She shook her head. "Only nineteen more days until Christmas. I can't wait until it's over." She scribbled numbers on a tag and fastened it to one of Treewing's branches.

Bewildered, Treewing glanced around. He saw a little white house on wheels and a busy street. Was this Christmas? Where were the ornaments, the families, and the happy children? Why had they taken his bird's nest away? What would happen to him now?

"Treewing! Treewing!" Treewing heard a voice call his name over and over. He woke from his sleep and looked up at a night that was not night. The stars were wrong. Hard and bright, they hung impossibly low on cords in long swooping lines, and they didn't twinkle. Pink, yellow, and blue triangular flags fluttered between them.

"Wake up, Treewing!"

17

Treewing looked over and saw Longbough standing in a wooden tree stand across from him.

"Longbough!" Treewing cried. "I'm so glad to see you!"

"And I you, my friend," Longbough said. "I'm so glad that Lolly moved me here across from you. When I heard in the giant truck that you'd been harvested, I hoped I'd see you again. What a miracle—"

"I like this tree, Daddy!" shouted a voice. A little boy in a red hat, jacket, and mittens ran down the row of trees and barreled into Longbough.

"Look out!" cried Longbough, swaying.

"My teddy bear likes this tree, too," the boy said, thrusting a stuffed bear into Longbough's branches. "See, Daddy?"

His father lifted Longbough's tag. "Nope. This one's too expensive." He glanced at Treewing. "And that one's shrimpy. Come on, Bradley. Let's go find a cheaper lot." He grabbed the boy's arm and pulled him away.

Longbough and Treewing stared at each other.

"What did he mean by 'too expensive'?" Treewing asked, hoping Longbough understood this strange place. After all, Longbough was a year older.

"I believe it means we are for sale," Longbough answered, his needles drooping. "And that man thought I cost too much. Preposterous! Absurd! Outrageous! I'm worth a great deal more, I am sure."

"But is all this—Christmas?"

"Wolves and icicles! I certainly hope not. The people appear to be choosing—like birds looking us over for a nesting place." He brightened, looking again like the old, laughing Longbough. "I have it! The songs say there is a special happy family for each of us. This," he gestured with one branch, "must be where they come to find us. It is merely a way station. We are still on our journey to Christmas."

"This isn't how I thought it would be," Treewing said.

"Neither did I. There are no stories or songs about this."

"Do you still believe in the Christmas Deer's promise?" Treewing blurted. "Still believe he is all wise?"

"Certainly!" Longbough rippled his needles. "How can you doubt him?"

Treewing felt ashamed, but doubt gnawed like a beaver at his bark.

"Don't worry, my little friend," Longbough said more gently. "We will find our homes. And remember, you have a 'special destiny.' I will wager a rainbow

there is more to that than just being harvested a year early. We simply have to wait—
wait and believe."

Four

Luke and Peacock

THE NEXT MORNING, Treewing woke early. Though the low brassy stars were pale now against the gray sky, they still shone with a dull light.

Beside him, Longbough stretched, his trunk creaking. "Wolves and icicles! How stiff I am!"

Treewing and Longbough were displayed at the front of the tree lot, and Treewing could see the little white house on wheels sitting near the entrance. Lolly came out with a broom and began sweeping pine and fir needles into piles. Cars whizzed by on the street. People scurried by on the sidewalk.

One woman, in an enormous blue coat with sleeves flapping like wings, pushed a shopping cart piled high with odds and ends. Jammed into one corner of the cart, waving over everything like a magic wand, was a peacock feather with an iridescent blue eye. Treewing watched it, fascinated. The woman stopped and looked at the trees. Lolly paused in her sweeping to glare at her. After giving Lolly a cheery wave, the woman walked away, one wheel on her shopping cart creaking.

So began Treewing's first full day in the Christmas tree lot. He dozed on and off, exhausted by the trip from Faith Mountain, by the shock of being harvested too soon, and by the unpleasant surprise of ending up in a world so different from the songs. In the middle of the afternoon, the street filled with children getting out of a nearby school. Some ran into the lot. A boy stopped in front of Treewing.

"Hi," the boy said. He was thin; his wrists stuck out of his brown jacket. Something bulged in the right pocket. He wore a baseball cap over his short acorn-colored hair. His green eyes peered out from beneath it.

"Who is he talking to?" Treewing asked Longbough. There were no other people in sight.

The boy blinked at Treewing. "You're small," he said, "like me. I'm the smallest boy in my class."

"He is talking to you, Treewing!" Longbough exclaimed.

"Can't be," said Barkcone, who stood in the frame beside Longbough. "People don't talk to trees."

"Hello," Treewing said to the boy. "Can you hear us?"

The boy tilted his head as if trying to catch some faint sound on the wind. He slipped off his red backpack and unzipped it. He pulled out a loop of gold yarn attached to a piece of purple construction paper shaped like a bell. Snakes of glue spangled with glitter squiggled across its front.

"It's a Christmas ornament," the boy explained. "A paper bell. I made it in school. I don't have a tree of my own to hang it on. So I guess I'll hang it on you, little tree." He slipped the red yarn loop over one of Treewing's branches. Then he stepped back and cocked his head to one side. "Perfect," he said.

The boy reached into his bulging jacket pocket and pulled out a baseball with red stitching scribbled with words in black marker. He rubbed his thumbs over it, then threw it up into the air. It made a slapping sound against his palm as he caught it with one hand. He threw it and caught it over and over again.

"My mom promised we'd have a place by Christmas," said the boy. "Have our own Christmas tree. But Christmas is almost here and we're still—"

A horn honked, and a battered silver van pulled up to the curb.

"Luke!" shouted a woman's voice.

"I gotta go," said the boy. He grabbed his backpack, ran across the parking lot, and jumped into the van.

The wind gusted, and the bell ornament on Treewing's branch flapped like an old crow.

"This isn't what the songs promised," Treewing whispered. "This isn't how I thought it would be."

Five

FIT FOR KINGS

"THE STARS HAVE spoken," said the woman in the enormous blue coat who had pushed the shopping cart earlier that day. "This is our tree." She was standing with another woman and a man in front of Treewing under the night sky. She touched the purple bell. "See, someone's already started decorating it."

"I don't know, Peacock," the man said, "it's kind of small. I bet you a toasted cheese sandwich a bigger tree would be better." He pulled on his black bow tie, which was torn on one end. "Are you sure?"

"The purple bell's a sign," Peacock said firmly. "This is our tree. No doubt about it."

"Treewing!" Longbough exclaimed. "They are going to take you home! Outstanding! Excellent! Fantastic!"

Treewing's bark quivered with joy. So he did have a special destiny after all! He was to be one of the first trees chosen.

"I have four itty-bitty candy canes they gave out at the shelter," said the other woman. Her frizzy red hair shot out from under her green stocking cap. She pulled four small candy canes wrapped in plastic out of her pocket and hung them on Treewing's branches.

Peacock clapped her hands—she had no gloves. "Marvelous, Mara! And I have some red yarn we can use for a garland. Found it in the dumpster behind Fabric Universe." She pulled the yarn out of her coat pocket and wound it through Treewing's branches.

"Your turn, David," Peacock said to the man with the torn bow tie. "What great offering do you have to bestow upon our noble tree?"

"Six silver gum wrappers," said David. "I'll just hang them over the branches." And he did.

"What are they doing?" Treewing asked Longbough, puzzled.

"I believe they are making a feeble attempt to decorate you," he said, laughing.

"But they're supposed to take me home first!"

"I am baffled, too. Baffled. Perplexed. Confounded."

"And those aren't proper ornaments," Barkcone scoffed. "Not like in the songs."

Treewing's heart fell. His boughs drooped. Just when his hopes had been raised, they had crashed down again.

"Oh, noble tree, we adorn thee," Peacock said. She tipped her head, considering Treewing. "Well, it's a start. We'll soon have this tree decorated fit for kings. We'd better leave before that Lolly sees us."

They walked back to the sidewalk, where Peacock had left her shopping cart. With the others following, she pushed it down the street, the front wheel on the cart creaking.

Early the next morning, Lolly passed Treewing as she was carrying a bucket through the lot. She stopped abruptly, stepped back, and stared at him.

"What on earth?" she said with a frown. Then a knowing look passed over her face. "Those homeless folk." She shook her

head. To Treewing's relief, she pulled off
the red yarn, the gum wrappers, the candy
canes, and the purple bell. "Trash," Lolly
said. She carried everything away in the
bucket.

Six

BILLY ANGELL

"LOOK OUT!" LONGBOUGH warned a few days later. "Here comes a shaker!" Treewing peered down the aisle. By now, so many people had inspected him that he only had to glance at them once to know exactly what they would do. Most simply lifted his tag and exclaimed,

"That much?" Or, "Who do they think they're kidding?" But many were suspicious, like the man down the aisle who was shaking Dewsylva to see if any of her needles fell off. Some people were spinners; they spun the trees around and around searching for hidden flaws. Lolly would follow them, muttering because they seldom bought anything. After they left, she would turn the trees so their best sides faced forward again, still muttering.

Once, a woman had spent two hours snapping her tape measure up and down the trees. Finally, she had chosen Mossbranch, a tall, elegant, noble fir.

"It will look simply delicious in the lobby," the woman had said, waving a plastic card at Lolly. "Do you deliver?"

Now, as Treewing watched poor Dewsylva shake, he heard the cries of "jollies" ring through the lot. Their cries would pass from tree to tree as they strolled down the aisles. The jollies—always a happy family with children—would crowd, oohing and aahing, laughing and chattering, around one lucky tree after another. Best of all, they usually took one home.

"Take me! Take me!" Treewing would whisper with all the others; for the jollies were what the trees had always imagined, what the songs had described. And Treewing believed his special destiny meant that a special family of jollies awaited him.

After the jollies chose a tree, Alicia would carry the lucky tree away while all the others cheered. But, Treewing noticed, Lolly never smiled or laughed, even after she had sold a tree.

"I'm glad you're still here," said Luke to Treewing the next afternoon. "We made bird ornaments today. A partridge in a pear tree, like in 'The Twelve Days of Christmas.'" Then Luke frowned. "What happened to my purple bell?"

"If only we could tell him," Treewing said to Longbough.

Luke hung the paper partridge ornament on one of Treewing's branches. The bird crouched in a little straw nest. Treewing felt a wave of homesickness for Faith Mountain.

"That looks pretty good," Luke said.

"It feels pretty good, too," Treewing said softly.

Luke stood back, took the baseball out of his pocket, and threw it up and down, catching it with one hand.

"Just what do you think you're doing?" said Lolly, appearing suddenly behind Luke.

"Oh dear," said Longbough. "Here comes trouble. Vexation. Bother."

Startled, Luke dropped the baseball. It rolled and stopped beside Lolly's feet. She picked it up. She turned it over in the heavy brown work gloves that covered her hands.

"This," she said, "this baseball,"—she stopped, then started again—"why, Billy Angell signed this ball."

"Sure did," said Luke proudly, pulling his baseball cap down lower on his head. "He's a pitcher for the Sandy Bay Stars. He won twenty-two games last season. And the Cy Young award. And his split-fingered fastballs are the best in the league. And—"

"I know who he is," Lolly interrupted. "I know all about him. Where'd you get this ball?"

"My dad gave it to me." Luke swallowed hard. "Just before he died."

"Poor boy," said Treewing. All of the trees sighed.

Lolly glanced up from the baseball. "How'd he die?"

"Car crash. Six months ago."

"'Shame," Lolly said. She looked back at the baseball. "My son, John, had a ball signed by Billy Angell. John died, too. In the war. Ten months, two weeks, and five days ago."

"Oh," said Luke. "I'm real sorry."

There was a silence.

"Can I have my baseball back, lady?" Luke asked.

"What?" Lolly said. "Oh." She hugged the baseball against her orange parka. "Oh," she said again. "Well, first you take that . . . that bird thing off that tree."

"No, don't!" Treewing cried. "I like it!"

But Luke removed the ornament.

Lolly turned the ball around and around in her hands, staring at it, then at last tossed it to Luke. "Now, you stay away from my lot. I got trees to sell, and I can't have them cluttered up with stuff. Decorate your tree at home."

"But I don't have one," Luke said. "Me and my mom live in our van."

"Not my problem," said Lolly. "Now, clear out."

Every night Peacock, Mara, David, and some of the other homeless people decorated Treewing with strange odds and ends from Peacock's shopping cart. They were nothing like the ornaments in the songs. All the other trees, except Longbough, made fun of him. To Treewing's relief, Lolly took down the decorations every morning.

Late one evening, Lolly and Alicia passed by Treewing after closing up.

"Only five more days until Christmas Eve," said Lolly. "We're going to have lots of unsold trees if we don't cut prices. And a lot of trees to dump."

"Dump!" Longbough roared.

"But if we lower prices now," Alicia said, "we'll barely break even."

"That's why I'm worried," Lolly said.

"Then let's wait two more days."

39

"All right," Lolly said. "But every tree that's still here day after tomorrow gets marked down." And they went into the trailer.

All over the lot, the trees cried out.

"Dumped!"

"But we're Christmas trees!"

"What about the Christmas Deer's promise?"

"How will dumping us bring The Return of Light?" asked Longbough.

Treewing's heart sank. Was it possible that Christmas would come and no star would crown his tip? No glittering glass ornaments or lights would illuminate his branches? No happy family of jollies would admire him? The Christmas Deer had promised that he had a special destiny. Treewing refused to believe that he would end up forgotten at the bottom of a dump.

Seven

THE 122ND BRIGADE

THE NEXT MORNING, beneath a glowering
gray sky, Treewing tried to look fresh and
magical for each person who walked past.
"Please," he whispered, "take me home." But
though the day dragged on, no one did. Only

a few trees spoke together; the horror of being dumped had cast a shadow over all of them.

That afternoon, Luke came walking toward Treewing, hands thrust deep in his jacket pockets. He stopped and gently touched one of Treewing's branches. Treewing quivered.

"Hi," said Luke. "I came to see if you'd been sold yet. I'm glad you're still here."

"He is glad!" said Longbough, outraged. "What a terrible thing to say."

But, to Treewing's surprise, he felt happy that he was still there for Luke. He hoped Luke would hang another bird ornament on him.

"You! Boy!" said Lolly, marching up. "I thought I told you to stay out of the lot."

Luke stepped back. "I—I didn't hang anything on him."

"Him?"

"This tree."

"What is it about this tree?" Lolly said, scowling. "All you homeless wanting to decorate it. I'd give anything never to see another blasted Christmas tree. Do you know what it's like, boy, when you want to block out everything about Christmas, every candy cane, ornament, present, tree, every single darned thing, but you can't 'cause you're in the Christmas business? You can't. You just can't." Her face crumpled.

"You just don't want Christmas without your son," Luke said softly.

"Bingo. Score one for you." Lolly looked at the pavement. "First Christmas without him."

"This is my first Christmas without my dad. He was in the war, too. The One hundred twenty-second Brigade out of Fort Home here in Sandy Bay. He was only back three months before the car crash."

Lolly glanced up. "John—my son—was in

the One hundred twenty-second."

They stared at each other.

"John took his baseball," Lolly said slowly, "the one signed by Billy Angell, with him to the war. He wanted to be a baseball player. Even had a spot lined up in the minors, but he wanted to serve his country first." She took a deep breath. "The ball didn't come home with his things after he died. I waited and waited for it, to have that piece of him back, but it didn't come." Lolly paused. Then she looked straight into Luke's eyes and whispered, "Where'd your dad get that ball?"

Luke swallowed. He put his hand in his pocket and clutched the ball. He looked at Treewing, then looked away.

"I don't know," he muttered.

"He does know," said Longbough. "He is just not telling."

"He's afraid," said Treewing. "But of what?"

A horn honked.

"I gotta go," said Luke. He ran to the street and stepped into the van. Lolly stared after him, the wind rippling the fringe of her pink muffler.

For the rest of the afternoon, the rain poured down. It dripped from one tier of Treewing's branches to the next, then *sput-spluttered* onto the pavement. It stopped when the sky turned dark, just in time for the evening shoppers. Soon afterward, an expectant cry rang through the lot: "Jollies! Jollies! Jollies!" Treewing straightened.

The family—a mother, father, two boys, and a girl—crowded around Longbough. The younger boy stuck his thumb in his mouth and rubbed his face in Longbough's branches. His sister tilted back her head, pointing stiffly with a hand swathed in a white mitten.

"We'll put Grandma's angel right there

on his tip," she said. "He's perfect."

"This tree's better," said the older boy, as he knelt beside Treewing. "Look. It's got a really long trunk, so you can fit more presents underneath."

Treewing, hoping as hard as he could, felt his branches shake.

"This one has a crooked tip," the father said, nodding toward Longbough. "And don't you think it's a bit overgrown, Michelle?

"Overgrown!" Longbough exclaimed.

Michelle tore her eyes away from the tip. "Oh no," she said. "He's wild. Like a tree in a fairy tale."

"An intelligent child," said Longbough. "Intelligent. Bright. Astute."

"But I don't have a crook in my tip," Treewing blurted.

"It is a curve!" Longbough exclaimed. "And my needles are greener than yours, my branches thicker, my whorls more evenly spaced. And I am older and bigger. I deserve to be a Christmas tree more than you."

Treewing's sap rose. "The Christmas Deer chose me specially!" he cried. "I'm more special than you!" Treewing suddenly hushed. What had he just said to his best friend? What had the strain of this terrible waiting, this creeping doubt, done to them both?

The older boy stood up from his crouch. "How do we decide which one to take?" he asked his mother.

"It has to be fair," Michelle said.

"Why not flip a coin?" Their mother took a quarter from her pocket. "If it's heads, we take this tree." She touched Longbough. "If it's tails, we take the other one. Agreed?"

"Okay," said all three children at once.

Their mother balanced the quarter on her thumbnail and forefinger, then with a *ping!* flicked it into the air. It spun up, flashing in the dark.

"Heads!" called Longbough, Michelle, and the younger boy.

"Tails," called Treewing and the older boy. The coin clattered on the pavement, bounced, rolled in a circle, wobbled, and finally fell flat. The children knelt beside it.

"Yes!" Michelle raised one arm. "It's heads!"

"I am going home with the jollies!" Longbough shouted.

Treewing stood silently, his branches sagging.

"I am sorry I shouted at you, Treewing," Longbough said. "Forgive me. Let us part as friends. Companions. Comrades."

"You'll always be my best friend," Treewing said, his boughs heavy, as he watched Lolly carry Longbough away.

Three days passed, three endless, lonely days for Treewing without Longbough. He hadn't realized how much he'd miss Longbough. "I have a special destiny," Treewing told himself over and over, but he was finding it harder and harder to believe. Then one afternoon Luke came walking toward him with something white and glittery in his hand. Treewing rippled his needles; he was glad to see Luke.

"I don't care what Lolly says, I'm hanging this star on you, little tree," Luke said to Treewing. He jumped up and hung a five-pointed, glittery white star on Treewing's tip.

"Treewing!" Barkcone exclaimed. "You almost look like a real Christmas tree!"

Treewing only sighed. He didn't believe anyone would ever choose him to be a real Christmas tree. His hopes were fading every day. Tomorrow was Christmas Eve, and Luke's star might be the only star that would ever hang on him. Though it was not made of crystal or silver or gold like the star ornaments in the songs, Treewing found he was grateful for it, nevertheless.

"Looks like Lolly has sold most of you trees," Luke said.

Treewing looked around the lot. It was true. Marking down the prices had done wonders for sales. There were only about two dozen trees left in the lot. But that was still two dozen trees who would be homeless on Christmas Day. Two dozen trees for whom the Christmas Deer's promise would be broken. Two dozen trees whose lives would not bring The Return of Light. Treewing shivered at the thought of the dump.

Luke pulled his baseball out of his pocket. "You know where my dad got this ball? From a guy in his brigade in the war. A friend gave it to him 'cause he knew how much my dad loved baseball—especially the Sandy Bay Stars. I wonder if it was Lolly's son, John. Just think. This could be Lolly's son's baseball." He closed his hand tight over the ball and shoved it back into his pocket.

"No," he said. "It's mine. My dad gave it to me. It's the last thing he ever gave me." And Luke whirled and walked away.

Eight

CHRISTMAS EVE

THE NEXT DAY was Christmas Eve day, and to Treewing's surprise, people swarmed about the lot choosing trees faster than Alicia and Lolly could load them onto cars and trucks. Treewing kept hoping that someone would want a small tree, but no one looked at him twice. Lolly, muttering, had removed Luke's star.

All day Treewing waited.

All day he hoped.

All day he prayed.

However, by nine o'clock on Christmas Eve, every tree in the lot had been sold—except him. All alone, he let his branches sag. The Christmas Deer had said he had a special destiny. Was this it? To be the only tree without a home or family? Oh, why hadn't he been left on Faith Mountain with the stars and the snowbirds? With everything he loved?

Alicia had gone home. Lolly was in her trailer. She had left the door open, and Treewing could see her sitting in a chair holding a framed picture in her hands. She had been sitting that way for some time.

The silver van pulled up to the curb, and Luke got out. He walked over to the trailer. When he saw Lolly sitting motionless, he stopped and watched her. His hand crept into his pocket, closing over the baseball. Lolly dropped the picture onto her lap and put her head in her hands. Luke kept watching her. Then, he walked a short distance away, turned, and walked back, whistling loudly.

Lolly looked up. She came out of the trailer.

"Oh, it's you," she said when she saw Luke. "What do you want?"

"Me and my mom were wondering if you had any spare boughs," Luke said. "We thought if we put some in our car, it would smell like Christmas." He glanced toward a big pile of broken branches in the back of the lot.

Lolly stared at him. "They're not free," she said at last.

"Why not?" said Luke. "You're just going to dump them tomorrow."

Treewing winced.

"Because this is a business. And a business

needs to make money. But I tell you what. You let me see that baseball of yours for a few minutes, and I'll give you six branches."

Luke clutched the baseball in his pocket. "No," he said.

"My son gave it to your dad, didn't he?" Lolly said softly.

"No. I mean, I don't know."

"Ask your mom."

"I did. Dad never told her the guy's name."

"I just want to see it," Lolly said. She looked away, tightened her pink muffler, and blinked hard. "Please," she whispered.

Treewing watched Luke's face turn stubborn. Then Lolly's face turned stubborn, too.

"No ball, no boughs," she said.

Luke didn't speak.

"Fine," she said. "I'm going to the supermarket."

"Fine," said Luke, and he walked back

to the silver van and got into it. Instead of pulling away, though, it stayed parked at the curb.

Lolly locked up the trailer and headed toward the supermarket.

Treewing looked at the empty tree stand where Longbough had stood. How he still missed his friend. Blown by the wind, a crumpled brown paper bag skittered aimlessly around the lot. Shadows crept out between the weeds growing in the cracks in the pavement.

"I'm just an ordinary little fir tree," Treewing whispered to the shadows, "the most common kind of Christmas tree. Not special after all. Nobody wants me. Just me, all alone on Christmas Eve." He sighed. "I'll be a Christmas tree for the wind. I'll count the stars. Remember Longbough laughing in the summer storms. And I *won't* think about tomorrow."

But although he tried and tried to be brave, Treewing felt his branches turn stiff, his needles brittle, and his thoughts dark.

Nine

THE RETURN OF LIGHT

A HALF HOUR LATER Peacock knocked on
the trailer door.

"She's not here," Treewing wanted to
tell her.

"Lolly's gone," Peacock said to David and
Mara, and to a group of four other people who
were with them. "With any luck, she's gone

for the night. Maybe to relatives to spend Christmas Eve. So let's get busy."

Pushing her shopping cart—the front wheel creaking, the peacock feather waving— she led the group toward Treewing. They stopped in front of him.

"How amazing," said Mara, "that out of all the trees in the lot, he's still here."

"It's a sign," said Peacock, nodding her head.

"I bet a toasted cheese sandwich it's going to snow," said David, pulling on his frayed bow tie.

"The shelter will be jammed," said Mara.

"We'll worry about that later," said Peacock. "Let's decorate, embellish, trim, adorn, bedeck." She started pulling things out of her shopping cart, her big blue sleeves swinging. "Mara, you wind the golden yarn around the tree as a garland. David, you tie these red twist ties onto its branches. Take these straws, Brittany and Eva. They're red and white, like candy canes—bendable, too. And Michael, Jason, use these crushed pop cans for ornaments. They'll shine like supernovas. Thread the branches through the pop-tops."

To Treewing's dismay, people started swarming around him, putting things on his branches. "Stop!" he wanted to tell them. "Don't put those strange things on me." Luke and his mother got out of the van and came over. Luke's mother wore a puffy, white parka with a wreath brooch pinned to it. She looked like a snowball.

"Merry Christmas," she said, smiling with bright magenta lips.

"What are you guys doing?" Luke asked Peacock.

"What's it look like?" Peacock said. "We're decorating our Christmas tree."

"Weird sort of decorations," Luke said, scratching his head under his baseball cap.

"We use what we have." Mara looped on the gold yarn.

"I decorated this tree, too," Luke said. "With a purple bell, a partridge, and a star. But Lolly threw them away—well, the bell and the star, anyway."

Peacock looked at him. "You made the purple bell? Cool. That's one reason we chose this tree in the first place. Want to help?"

Luke looked at his mother. "Can I?"

"Sure," she said. "Do you want to contribute the paper chain you made that's on the dashboard?"

Luke nodded. "I'll run and get it." He came back a minute later with a six-foot long paper chain made out of red, green, and silver loops of shiny paper.

"Divine!" Peacock exclaimed. "Start at the top and work your way down."

Someone began singing "Deck the Halls with Boughs of Holly," and they all joined in while they decorated Treewing. It was crisp and cold, and a few snowflakes fell, like one quick shake from a saltshaker. Luke's paper chain glittered on Treewing's boughs. At least there is something glittering on me for Christmas Eve, Treewing thought. Something shiny. Something sparkly. Thanks to Luke. Then Treewing realized the crushed pop cans were shiny, too. Maybe they weren't so bad, maybe. . . .

"Stop!" called an angry voice. "Just stop what you're doing. Stop this minute."

The group of people parted, and Lolly stepped through, carrying a plastic bag full of groceries, her face red. Her eyes were red, too, as though she'd been crying.

"You're trespassing on private property,"

she said. "The bunch of you. Take all this . . . this garbage off that tree and clear off."

"But you're not going to sell him," Luke said. "So what's it hurting?"

"Hurting?" Lolly asked. "Hurting? I'm hurting, that's what. I don't like Christmas, do you understand me? I can't stand it. Not without John here. What's it hurting? Clear out!" she shouted. "Clear out now or I'll call the police!"

"But we like this tree," said Peacock. "It cheers us up. We need it, and so do you, Lolly."

Treewing stood perfectly still. They needed him? Bells pealed through the frosty air as the church clocks struck twelve. They needed him? Yes, he finally understood. They needed him to bring them The Return of Light.

"Oh, Christmas Deer," he whispered, "*this* is my special destiny, isn't it?"

Treewing looked at the people. "You are *my* family," he said. "It is *you* who are special. Decorate me with whatever brings you happiness. I will be your Christmas tree."

Then, as Treewing remembered the Christmas Deer touching him with his starry antlers, he felt a spark deep down inside. It grew until light blazed through him, tingling over his needles, skipping and dancing along his boughs, until he glowed from trunk to tip. He could feel his roots again up on the mountain. The ringing bells filled the air with glory.

"Look! Look!" exclaimed Mara. "The Christmas tree is shining with light!"

Luke stared at Treewing. Then he smiled. A brilliant smile, Longbough would have said. Brilliant. Dazzling. Radiant.

Luke stepped forward and took his baseball out of his pocket. Lolly's eyes snapped to it. Luke turned the ball in his hands. He opened his mouth and closed it again. He swallowed hard. "Billy Angell," he said at last. Luke held the ball out to Lolly. "I think this belonged to your son. You should have it. My dad would want you to have it. So do I."

Luke's mother nodded.

As though in a dream, Lolly set down her bag of groceries. She held out both pink-gloved hands, and Luke dropped the baseball into them. "Merry Christmas," he said. Lolly stared at him, and a smile dawned on her lips, growing bigger and bigger until her whole face was bright.

"The Return of Light!" Treewing shouted.

Peacock, David, and Mara joined hands, as did all the other homeless people. Luke's mother took Luke's hand. He took Peacock's free hand. People on their way home from Christmas Eve church services saw Treewing shining magically and mysteriously, and they also joined the group. Cars passing on the street stopped. The people inside the cars got out, and they, too, joined the group until there were at least fifty people all holding hands.

As the snow began to fall in earnest, Lolly, standing between the crowd and Treewing, stepped forward and placed the baseball under Treewing.

"This tree stays up until New Year's," she called out. "He'll be the Christmas Tree for everyone who doesn't have one."

The crowd cheered. Then Lolly turned toward the group. She stepped between Luke and Peacock, taking their hands. A couple began to sing "Silent Night," and everyone else chimed in.

Adorned with a paper chain, red twist ties, golden yarn, straws, and crushed pop cans, Treewing glowed and glowed, love and joy beaming out from him into the crowd. Brightest of all was the star of light crowning his tip, crowning him as a Christmas tree for everyone, a Christmas tree who had brought The Return of Light.